POETRY

by

Aida Levonian-Tonoyan

First Edition

Fulton Books, Inc.
Meadville, PA

First originally published by Fulton Books 2018

ISBN 978-1-63338-490-3 (Paperback)
ISBN 978-1-63338-491-0 (Digital)

Printed in the United States of America

This book is dedicated to all
the children in the world

Acknowledgments

I would like to express my gratitude to my dear friend Dan Wood (professor of English), who, despite his extremely busy schedule, found time and interest to read and edit my poems.

The painting above the aquarium in "Snowball the Cat" is my friend, Betty B. K.'s, stolen artwork. The loss of it saddened us both so much that I decided to include the photo of it in my book.

Contents

The Fly 6
The Squirrel 7
Piggy 9
The First Day of School 10
Smart Father 11
Snowball the Cat 12
The Metal Plane 13
The Magic Hat 14
Chubby Alex 15
The Piano 16
The Tulip 17
Vacation by the Sea 18
The Magical Sailboat 19
The Nest 20
The Lesson 21
The Naughty Wind 22
The Sudden Rain 24
Don't Rush 26
Nasty Gossip 27
Soup 28
Laundry 29
The Rainbow Garden 30
The Enchanted Garden 31

The Fly

A fuzzy fly, to great alarm,
Got in and sat right on my arm,
Then bravely landed on my head,
And even tried to taste my bread!

It flew in circles, smelled the pot.
The stew inside was steaming hot!
Back toward me the creature flew.
To him said I, "With you I'm through!"

I tried to chase the fly away,
Yet it kept staring at my tray.
The naughty thing dared
come so close,
It even landed on my nose!

I gulped my stew, which still was hot.
Share my good food? Certainly not!
I swallowed everything so fast,
The little pest was left to fast!

The Squirrel

O fluffy squirrel, come join me please,
To clean the leaves under these trees.
With your great speed and fuzzy tail
I'm sure, my pal, we will not fail.

I promised dad to clean the yard,
And with your help it won't be hard.
I played all day and soon forgot,
Ignored small tasks become a lot.

I'll treat you well for your good deed
And give you apricots, indeed,
And any time you pass this way,
I will not chase my friend away.

CHRIS

Piggy

I am Piggy, I am pink.
My curly tail is like a spring.
I can eat all day and night,
Yet my stomach still feels light.

Soy beans, veggies, fruits and meat,
Plants and flowers, corn and wheat—
I eat everything with ease,
Just give me food! I'm hungry, please!

With the help of my flat snout
I'll find the food without a doubt.
My sense of smell is very strong,
Finding food does not take long.

Eating isn't all I do,
I care a lot for music too.
But most of all I like to play
With little kids that pass my way.

And why do people always think
That pigs are dirty and they stink?
The muddy puddles keep us cool,
But I prefer a nice, clean pool.

The First Day of School

Whose voice is screaming in the yard?
It's little Steven crying hard.
In his preschool he wants to stay,
But elementary school? No way!

The caring neighbors gathered fast,
And frightened Steven soon relaxed.
They greeted him with an embrace
Which put a smile upon his face.

Steve made new friends, had lots of fun,
In his new school his fear was gone!
The next day's sun, observed our boy
Run fast to school with pride and joy!

Smart Father

I just hate to wake up for school in the morning.
The disturbing alarm sounds harsh and annoying.
It's so cozy in bed, and I struggle to rise,
But it takes so much strength just to open my eyes.

"It won't be a torment getting up with the sun
If you go to bed early, my dear, young son."
I respect my father, he is so kind and wise!
Whenever we need it, he will always advise!

Snowball the Cat

Fluffy Snowball, set me free,
You can't come to skate with me.
Stay at home, catch playful mice,
But don't hurt them, just be nice.

And remember, by the way,
With my fish you cannot play!
When I'm back, I'll give you milk
And brush your fur—fine as silk.

Here, pal, catch this tennis ball,
Just don't crash into a wall.
Oh, my funny little cat,
I adore you, you know that!

Even though, at busy times
You do bother me sometimes.
I can't play with you all day,
Yet you never stay away.

You jump up on my desktop,
Dropping books with flip and flop.
I have schoolwork, can't you see?
Lucky kitty, you are free.

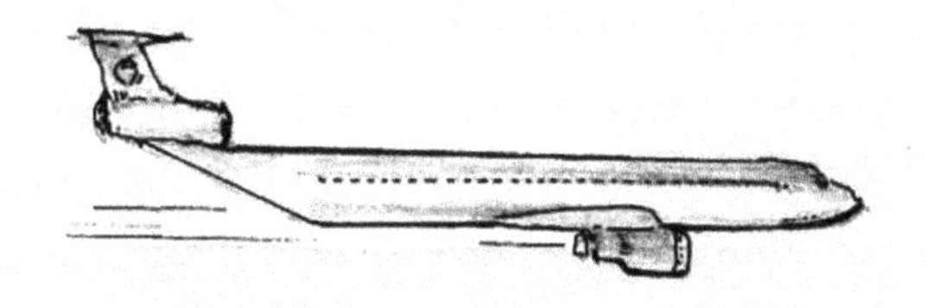

The Metal Plane

I'm flying in an airplane—
It's so serene below.
The clouds resemble cotton,
Or maybe fields of snow.

Before, when I was younger,
I was afraid to fly.
I would try to hide my fear,
And no one saw me cry.

My uncle on my birthday
Gave me a metal plane.
I liked it even better
Than my beloved train.

My friends and many neighbors
Would come and stand in line,
And each of them desired
To have a plane like mine.

I am brave and older now,
And I no longer cry.
I gave my plane to Tommy
Who's also scared to fly.

The Magic Hat

I wish I had a magic hat
To make me disappear.
I could scare the bully Jason
And whisper in his ear.

I could use it during soccer
To quickly kick some goals.
The surprised goalie
would be shocked
While standing at the poles!

I could become a stealthy spy
And sneak in anywhere,
Uncover secrets, save the world
From bad guys everywhere.

I could accomplish lots of good,
I even felt some pride,
But then I thought,
"How could I hide
From those mean dogs outside?"

Of course, you cannot
hide from beasts!
They'd smell you right away.
My dream has ended oh so fast,
Yet, I had fun today!

Chubby Alex

My friend Alex is depressed,
He is feeling very stressed.
No one wants him on their team,
"We will lose with him!"
they scream.

"He is fat and runs so slow,
That our scores will be too low."
Who can help or give advice?
Alex ran to Doctor Brice.

"If you want to lose some weight,
Get the junk food off your plate,
Move a lot and exercise,
That's the best I can advise."

Alex followed his advice,
Ate more veggies and less rice.
All those pastries and those sweets
Were replaced with fruits and beets.

Alex changed, so no more tears.
He plays soccer with his peers.
He is cheerful, and he's fun.
He can now jump and run!

The Piano

In the far corner of the room
My brown piano stands in gloom.
It looks so lonely and obscure,
We have neglected it for sure.

But when I sit with great desire
And on the keys play Haydn's "Fire,"
It comes alive, awakens all,
And shakes the pictures in the hall.

It shoots the notes up in the air,
Igniting hearts with magic flare,
And glitters gorgeously with pride,
Content and happy, like a bride.

The Tulip

I planted a tulip bulb in a pot,
Then watered the soil,
and sang from my heart:
"My dear red tulip,
I'll take care of you,
I'll protect you from mice,
and water you, too."

A month passed so quickly,
it's already May.
I've been watching my flower
day after day.
My work was not wasted,
and my tulip soon
Bloomed quite gorgeously
in the middle of June.

The neighbors would stop,
and for a moment stand still,
To admire the flower
on my windowsill.
With its graceful petals
and magnificent style,
My beautiful tulip
cheered us all with a smile.

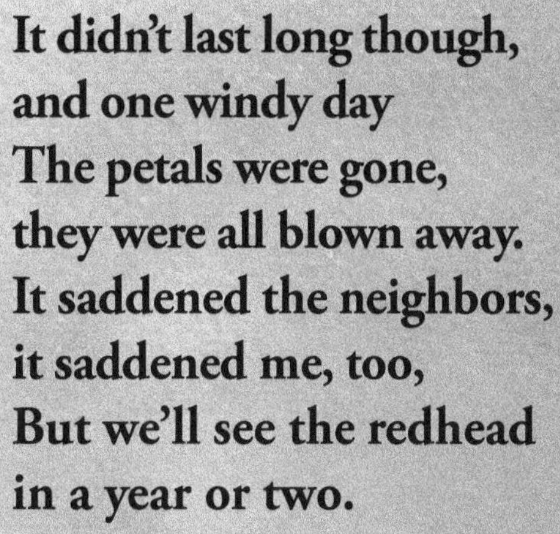

It didn't last long though,
and one windy day
The petals were gone,
they were all blown away.
It saddened the neighbors,
it saddened me, too,
But we'll see the redhead
in a year or two.

Vacation by the Sea

I wait for my summer vacation to start
To rush to the beach and see Grandfather Bart.
The fresh air, golden sun, warm sand, and the sea,
With its salty water, are waiting for me.

I walk on the beach and dig shells in the sand,
And watch the ships sailing away from dry land.
I observe seagulls spotting fish from up high
And happy children flying kites in the sky.

The waves hit the rocks and then pull back in vain
Prepared to attack the stone giants again.
The light breeze flows gently, caressing my hair,
And carries the scent of the sea in the air.

Suntanned, refreshed, and with a great deal of zest,
At vacation's end I'll interrupt my quest.
With beautiful shells and fun stories to tell,
To home I'll return feeling vibrant and swell.

The Magical Sailboat

Magical sailboat,
Let me sail with you.
I'd like very much
To see the world too.

Let the wind blow us
To north, east, and west,
And then in the south
We will end our quest.

Let's follow swallows
And see where they land,
Discover beaches
Of pink-colored sand.

Let's study the stars
In the pitch-black sky,
Watch playful dolphins—
They jump up so high!

And when we are tired
And homesick, my friend,
Just take me back home—
Our roving will end.

The Nest

A sparrow built a nest
in spring
On our porch one day.
It laid five eggs in it, and soon
The birdies hatched, all gray.

Now every morning—tweet,
tweet, tweet!
Their chirping wakes me up.
Their exciting loud noises
Seem endless and nonstop.

The mother carries worms for them,
The birdies quickly snatch.
The nimble ones are always fast,
And are the first to catch.

"There's always plenty food around,"
Assures the sparrow-mom.
But the young, impatient birdies
Can't possibly stay calm.

The sparrow-birdies soon will grow
And learn to find their food.
They will fly up into the trees
And leave their nest for good.

There, in the bushes and the trees
The sparrow-birds will pair,
And in the spring they will build nests
And have a home to share.

The Lesson

The plains are green, it's spring around!
The sun's rays gently warm the
ground,
The grass smells fresh, the sky is clear,
It's beautiful and peaceful here!

The birds are gathering some twigs
To build their nests and
have their chicks.
The butterflies in graceful flights
Bring nature's colors to new heights.

Sheep are grazing in the meadow,
Their shepherd—a tall young fellow
Has brought with him two giant dogs
To watch the flock like
sharp-eyed hawks
And to make sure that all is well.
There could be danger, who can tell?

A careless ewe got lost one day,
Into dark woods she slipped away.
The poor thing grasped a little late
That she was lost and left to fate.

Some wolves appeared from out of
sight,
The lamb got scared, she couldn't fight.
She started trembling from great fear,
But luckily, the dogs were near.

The hungry beasts were chased away,
The lamb by chance was saved that day.
She learned her lesson after that
And only grazed where guard dogs sat.

The Naughty Wind

Naughty wind, you're back again!
I just swept the porch in vain!
You show up, and right away
Chaos follows in your way.

With a mighty howl you blow,
Uprooting plants as you go!
You lift dust up in the air,
Creating storms everywhere!

Throwing pine cones from tall trees,
Frightens all the squirrels and bees!
Tearing petals, ripping leaves,
Causes damage, stop it, please!

Also, you mess up my hair!
I don't miss you, be aware.
Watch your temper, don't be mad!
Enough, wind, you make me sad!

Can you be a little nice
And surprise us just for once!?
Blow that grandma with her sack
Gently home on her way back.

CHRIS

The Sudden Rain

I love to read in our backyard,
Especially in May.
The pleasant weather lures us out
To freshen up and play.

The lively birds chirp merrily
And fly from tree to tree.
The roses look so heavenly,
One's spirit sings from glee.

In the gazebo, one nice day,
Enjoying my new book,
I looked around, and suddenly
The place had changed its look.

The noisy children had gone home,
The bright sun disappeared,
I could not hear the birds or bees,
Gray clouds above appeared.

And suddenly a heavy rain
Poured rushing from the sky.
I badly wanted to run home,
But will my book stay dry?

The heavy rain did not last long.
I was relieved to see
That my new book did not get wet,
It was a gift to me.

Don't Rush

My grandma Nancy has aged more;
She's not as active as before.
Her pretty auburn hair turned gray,
And she is changing day by day.

Her smooth face with two cute dimples
Has brought forth a few new wrinkles.
Her posture is no longer straight.
She can't walk fast, and she's gained
weight.

She sees the photos of her past
And sighs . . . her life went by so fast.
Nevertheless, despite it all,
My life with granny is a ball!

I love my grandma's graceful style,
Her lovely face, and her soft smile.
My days with her are always bright;
She is my angel and my light!

A grown young man I rush to be,
But grandma tells me, "Live carefree!
Your youthful years will pass by fast;
Enjoy them, sweetheart,
while they last."

I laugh and play with friends today,
And don't feel bad in any way.
The words of wisdom grandma said,
I'll carry always in my head.

Nasty Gossip

Penny was gossiping—it's something that we hate!
To spread rumors and lies around she could not wait.
Whatever she heard, she quickly told everyone.
The girl liked to gossip, and she thought it was fun.

Like a boomerang's throw, life may get you someday.
A bumble bee stung Penelope's tongue one day.
"Hurray, the gossip girl cannot talk anymore!"
And the happy news rapidly went door to door.

The laughter and thrill of all the people around
Quite embarrassed Penny, and she dropped to the ground.
The neighbors only wanted the young girl to see
How unpleasant and painful one's gossip can be.

The fault was recognized, and so from that day on,
The gossiping stopped, and all the tension was gone.

Soup

I decided with Fay to impress our friends
And invite them for soup today, at school's end.
We ran to the market to purchase some stuff
And, not to be short, we bought more than enough.

We bought onion heads and red beets for the stew,
Tomatoes, and carrots—a cabbage head, too.
A bag of potatoes we purchased for us,
Grabbed some sweets for dessert, and came home on the bus.

We chopped the washed veggies and mixed them in haste,
Then added some butter and spices to taste,
Placed it all in a pot and covered it up,
And while the soup cooked, we had time to cleanup.

Together with Fay, we picked up everywhere,
Set nicely the table, and fixed up our hair.
We washed all the dishes and mopped up the floor,
And soon came our friends with a knock on the door.

The soup smelled delicious, and I with much grace
Showed the guests to the table with a proud face.
My smile disappeared when I looked in the pot.
We forgot the water! I froze on the spot!

Laundry

I love my mom, she cares for me.
She's always busy, never free.
As a surprise for Mother's Day,
I thought to wash our
clothes that day.

I got the towels, socks, and shirts,
My mother's dresses,
pants, and skirts.
I gathered all, the slippers too,
The laundry pile just grew and grew.

I pressed it all in the machine,
Poured soap and bleach
to wash it clean,
Read the instructions,
pressed the knob,
Left the machine to do its job.

The wash was done, and
with some haste,
Into the dryer all I placed.
My task is done! Hurray! Hurray!
My mom will be so thrilled today!

It's true that mothers never rest,
Their work is endless, they are stressed.
We need to offer help sometimes
And do some chores at busy times.

My mother soon returned at last.
She saw the laundry, and she gasped.
I guess I didn't do too well.
She turned all white and almost fell!

The Rainbow Garden

When the heavy rain stopped
And the sun shone up high,
A colorful rainbow
Appeared high in the sky.

But it did not last long
And soon, fading away,
It was suddenly gone,
As if it could not stay.

An idea occurred
In my youthful head fast:
"I can plant a rainbow,
And it would be a blast!"

When the weather warmed up
And soon spring came around,
I took up the shovel
To start digging the ground.

In all seven colors
I planted my flowers
And completed the work
After several hours.

Many months have gone by,
I have waited so long,
But there was no rainbow,
Surely, something was wrong.

Through excitement and haste
I just failed to recall
That the bloom time for plants
Is quite different for all.

The Enchanted Garden

The garden is stunning when it is in bloom.
The fragrant white roses smell just like perfume.
The butterflies, lively with colorful wings,
Are treated by flowers as if they were kings.

The bright-colored petals allure them with winks
And serve them refreshing and nourishing drinks.
The elegant daisies, white clovers, florets
Are quite proudly standing to welcome their guests.

The charming insects are enjoying the sun,
In their pretty short lives, they are having some fun.
The garden's enchanted like heaven in May,
With butterfly-angels adorning the day.

CPSIA information can be obtained
at www.ICGtesting.com
Printed in the USA
BVHW091102110319
542318BV00019B/1517